A NOTE TO PARENTS

When your children are ready to "step into reading," giving them the right books—and lots of them—is as crucial as giving them the right food to eat. **Step into Reading Books** present exciting stories and information reinforced with lively, colorful illustrations that make learning to read fun, satisfying, and worthwhile. They are priced so that acquiring an entire library of them is affordable. And they are beginning readers with an important difference—they're written on four levels.

Step 1 Books, with their very large type and extremely simple vocabulary, have been created for the very youngest readers. **Step 2 Books** are both longer and slightly more difficult. **Step 3 Books,** written to mid-second-grade reading levels, are for the child who has acquired even greater reading skills. **Step 4 Books** offer exciting nonfiction for the increasingly proficient reader.

Children develop at different ages. **Step into Reading Books,** with their four levels of reading, are designed to help children become good—and interested—readers *faster*. The grade levels assigned to the four steps—preschool through grade 1 for Step 1, grades 1 through 3 for Step 2, grades 2 and 3 for Step 3, and grades 2 through 4 for Step 4—are intended only as guides. Some children move through all four steps very rapidly; others climb the steps over a period of several years. These books will help your child "step into reading" in style!

To Lauren at two

Library of Congress Cataloging-in-Publication Data:
Dubowski, Cathy East. Cave boy. (Step into reading. A Step 1 book) SUMMARY: A cave boy gives his grumpy chief something previously unseen for his birthday—and makes him smile. [1. Cave dwellers—Fiction] I. Dubowski, Mark, ill. II. Title. III. Series: Step into reading. Step 1 book. PZ7.D8544Cav 1988 [E] 87-23427 ISBN: 0-394-89571-1 (pbk.); 0-394-99571-6 (lib. bdg.)

Manufactured in the United States of America   10

STEP INTO READING is a trademark of Random House, Inc.

Step into Reading

CAVE BOY

By Cathy East Dubowski and Mark Dubowski

A Step 1 Book

Random House New York

Hi.

My name is Harry.

I live with my family

in this cave.

My friends like to
run and jump
and swing and climb.
I like those things too.

But most of all
I like to make new things.
Things no one has
ever seen before.

I put a rock on a stick.
What does it do?

Bam! Bam!
I call it a bammer.

I cut up a log.

What does it do?

Boom! Boom!

I call it a boomer.

"Stop all that bamming!
Stop all that booming!"

That is Chief Grump.
He is always mad
about something.

Tomorrow is his birthday.
Maybe I can
cheer him up.

I will make something new,
just for Chief Grump.

Wow!

I have never seen

anything like it!

My friends say,
"What is that thing?"
I say, "Don't look!
It is a surprise!"

It is time for
Chief Grump's party.

He gets lots
of presents.
A rock, some wood,
a fish, a bone.

Chief Grump says,
"I do not need this!
I do not want that!"
He throws them
down the hill.

Now Chief Grump
opens my present.
"What does it do?"

Everyone looks
at my new thing.
"Does it bam or boom?"
"Does it bounce?"
"Does it bite?"

But no one can guess
what it does.
Not even me.

Chief Grump says,
"It does not do
anything!"

He kicks it
down the hill.

Hey!
Now I know what
this new thing does.

It rolls!

I take it back to my room.

I put something here.

I add something there.

Maybe Chief Grump
will like it now.

I tell him,
"Sit here.
Put your feet there."
I give him a push.

Look! I made something
really new.
Something no one
has ever seen before.

I made
Chief Grump smile!